Cat Napped!

LEEZA HERNANDEZ

G. P. Putnam's Sons • An Imprint of Penguin Group (USA)

G. P. PUTNAM'S SONS
Published by the Penguin Group
Penguin Group (USA) LLC
375 Hudson Street
New York, NY 10014

USA | Canada | UK | Ireland | Australia
New Zealand | India | South Africa | China
penguin.com
A Penguin Random House Company

Library of Congress Cataloging-in-Publication Data
Hernandez, Leeza, author, illustrator.
Cat napped! / Leeza Hernandez.
pages cm
Summary: A lost pet cat finds her way home with help from a kindly passerby
and the animal shelter. [1. Cats—Fiction. 2. Lost and found possessions—Fiction.]
I. Title. II. Title: Catnapped!   PZ7.H431777Cat 2014   [E]—dc23   2013022383

Manufactured in China by South China Printing Co. Ltd.
ISBN 978-0-399-16438-5
10 9 8 7 6 5 4 3 2 1

Design by Annie Ericsson.
Text set in Zapatista.
The illustrations are rendered in pencil, with hand-painted textures of watercolor
and acrylic paints on paper, which are then scanned and collaged digitally.

For Jo Morrison
and all the kitties at
Cats Protection, Isle of Wight.

Kitty cat.

Pretty cat.

Living in the city cat.

Mosey cat.

Nosey cat.

Curl up nice
and cozy cat.

BARGAIN
ITEMS
$2.50

Shake cat.

Quake cat.

There must be
some mistake cat.

Dash cat.

Crash cat.

Colliding with
the trash cat.

Cries a hurt
"MEEEE-OWL!" cat.

Found cat.

Surround cat.

Taken to the pound cat.

Gray cat?

Stray cat?

One came in today cat.

Huddle cat.

Cuddle cat.

What a silly muddle cat.

Wrap cat.

Lap cat.

The only way to nap cat.

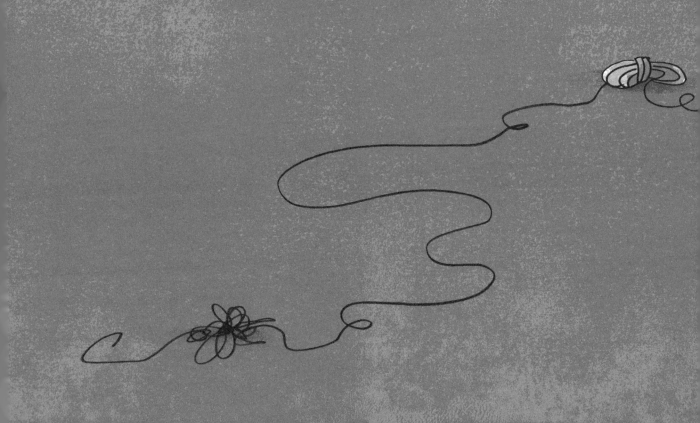